For Dreamers everywhere – RLS
For Susie – DS

First published in the United Kingdom in 2003 by
The Chicken House, 2 Palmer Street, Frome, Somerset, BA11 1DS
www.doublecluck.com
This edition published in 2004

Designed by Ian Butterworth

Printed and bound in Singapore

British Library Cataloguing in Publication data available
Library of Congress Cataloguing in Publication data available

ISBN: 1 904442 25 0

The Sheep Fairy

When Wishes Have Wings

By
Ruth Louise Symes

Illustrated by
David Sim

The Chicken HOUSE

This is Wendy Woolcoat. Wendy likes:

eating grass

eating grass

eating grass

eating grass

eating grass

eating grass

eating grass

eating grass

eating grass

eating grass

sleeping

eating grass

eating grass

eating grass

eating grass

eating grass

One day Wendy was eating grass when a tiny voice said,

"Help me! Please, help me."

It was a fairy, stuck in a brambly bush.

Wendy was a kind sort of sheep, so she ate all the brambles around the fairy and set her free.

"Oh thank you," said the fairy.
"As a special reward for helping
me I'll give you one wish.
What would you like?"

"Well," said Wendy, thinking hard.
"Best of all I like eating grass and
then I like sleeping."

"But you can do both of those already," said the fairy. "There must be something else you dream about?"

"Oh that!" said Wendy. She'd never told anyone about her secret dream before, so she told the fairy, very quietly.

"Speak up!" the fairy said. "I can't hear you."

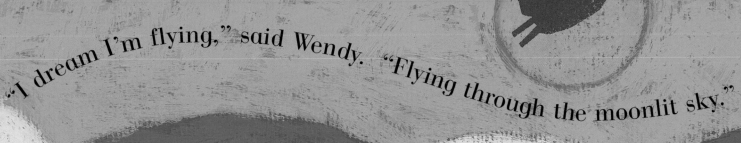

"I dream I'm flying," said Wendy. "Flying through the moonlit sky."

Wendy looked round quickly to see if any of the other sheep had heard her. They all had their heads down, eating grass. Wendy started to eat grass too. It was delicious.

"When the moon comes up and the stars come out, your wish will come true," said the fairy, as she flew off.

But Wendy was much too busy eating grass to listen.

When the moon came up and the stars came out,
Wendy had a very strange feeling indeed.

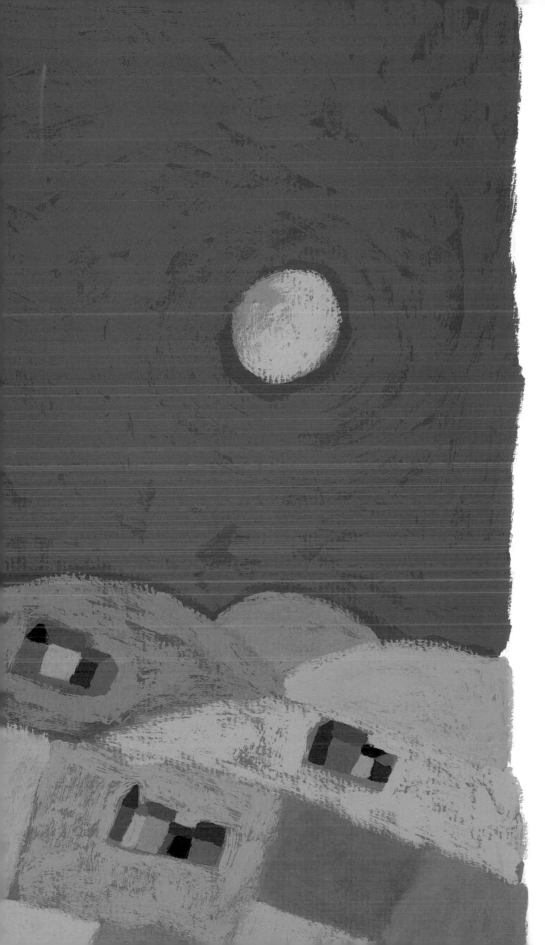

She
felt
like
she
was
floating
upwards.

The field was far below.

"Baa," Wendy bleated to the other sheep and she wiggled her legs about as if she was running in the sky.

On her back Wendy had grown a pair of beautiful sheep–sized fairy wings. She flapped them up and down, "Baa baa baa, look at me – I'm flying!" But the other sheep were fast asleep.

She soon got the
hang of flying:

forwards

backwards

upwards

downwards

in loop the loops

in figures of 8

Wendy flew over the
farmer's house and over
the town and out to sea.

Flying was wonderful. It was even better than she'd dreamt it could be.

On the way back Wendy saw a wolf strolling down the lane towards the sheep's field.

"Wake up, wake up, there's a wolf coming!" Wendy cried. But the sheep carried on sleeping. "Wake up, wake up, there's a wolf coming – and he's coming to get you!"

But the sheep still didn't wake up and it was almost too late. The wolf was in the sheep's field. Wendy had to do something!

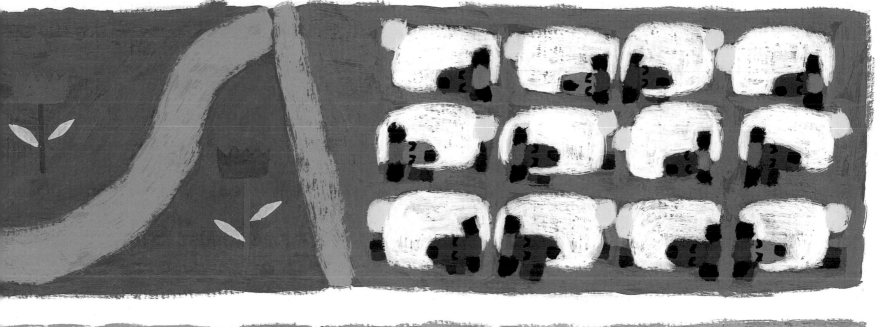

Wendy flew straight at the wolf.
"Leave my friends alone!"
she shouted.

The next morning the sheep in Wendy's field
were doing what they did every morning:

eating grass

eating grass

eating grass

eating grass

"I had a really strange dream last night," said Sheep 1.

"Me too," said Sheep 2.

"Me three," said Sheep 3.

And all the other sheep agreed. "Baa baa baaa."

"I dreamt that Wendy could fly."

"That's what I dreamt."

"And me."

"And us. Baa."

But when they went to ask Wendy,
she was fast asleep.

A new clutch of picture books from The Chicken House!

A Secret in the Garden
illustrated by James Mayhew

A beautiful hide-and-seek picture book inspired by the classic story,
The Secret Garden by Frances Hodgson Burnett. Perfect for children of all ages.

ISBN: 1 904442 24 2
£5.99

Pudding
written by Pippa Goodhart and illustrated by Caroline Jayne Church

A warm and comforting story about making friends.

ISBN: 1 904442 02 1
£5.99

The Children's Book of Alphabets
introduced by Wendy Cooling

A beautiful collection of new and favourite alphabet verses and rhymes
showing some of the many different ways children can enjoy learning and
playing with letters. A treasury for every nursery bookshelf.

ISBN: 1 904442 10 2
96 pages   £5.99

Visit our Internet site **www.doublecluck.com** for more details of Chicken House titles.
Prices and availability are subject to change.

Like all sheep, Wendy spends most of her life eating and sleeping. But Wendy has a secret dream, and when she rescues a fairy caught in a bramble bush, her life changes for ever.

A story about wishes with wings and dreams that really do come true!

The Chicken House

£5.99

ISBN 1-904442-25-0

9 781904 442257

www.doublecluck.com